THE LITTLEST VOYAGEUR

THE
LITTLEST
VOYAGEUR

Margi Preus

Pictures by
Cheryl Pilgrim

MARGARET FERGUSON BOOKS
HOLIDAY HOUSE · NEW YORK

The publisher wishes to thank Stephen Veit,
museum technician at Grand Portage National Monument,
and Linda LeGarde Grover for their expert help.

Margaret Ferguson Books
Text copyright © 2020 by Margi Preus
Illustrations copyright © 2020 by Cheryl Pilgrim
All Rights Reserved
HOLIDAY HOUSE is registered in the U.S. Patent and Trademark Office.
Printed and bound in December 2019 at Maple Press, York, PA, USA.
www.holidayhouse.com
First Edition
1 3 5 7 9 10 8 6 4 2

Canoe Manned by Voyageurs Passing a Waterfall by Frances Anne Hopkins
used by permission of Library and Archives Canada / accession number
1989-401-1 / e011153912, C-002771

Library of Congress Cataloging-in-Publication Data
Names: Preus, Margi, author. | Pilgrim, Cheryl, illustrator.
Title: The littlest voyageur / Margi Preus ; illustrated by Cheryl Pilgrim.
Description: First edition. | New York : Margaret Ferguson Books, Holiday
House, [2020] | Summary: In 1792, Jean Pierre Petit Le Rouge, a squirrel,
eager for adventure, stows away in the canoe of a group of voyageurs,
unaware of what they are traveling so far to trade. Includes pronunciation
guide, historical notes, and a recipe. | Includes bibliographical references.
Identifiers: LCCN 2019009423 | ISBN 9780823442478 (hardcover)
Subjects: | CYAC: Adventure and adventurers—Fiction. | Fur traders—Fiction.
| Squirrels—Fiction. | Canada—History—18th century—Fiction.
Classification: LCC PZ7.P92434 Lit 2020 | DDC [Fic]—dc23
LC record available at https://lccn.loc.gov/2019009423

To all who work to preserve and protect
our wilderness annd waterways
— M. P.

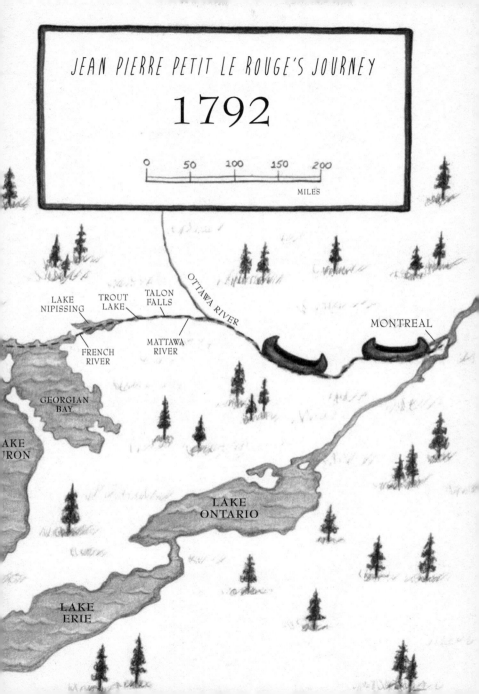

THE LITTLEST VOYAGEUR

PART I
THE VOYAGE

MY WANDERLUST IS BORN

The flash of red paddles.

The sound of strong, singing voices.

I leapt to a higher branch for a better view of the mighty Ottawa River.

Canoe after canoe after canoe—a whole brigade of canoes—moved along the waterway below my treetop home. Each big birch-bark canoe loaded with many bundled parcels. Each propelled by a crew of eight to twelve voyageurs.

Each voyageur paddling like mad. And singing!

I sang a song, too: "Come back! I want to go with you!"

No answer.

I flung myself from branch to branch, trying to catch up with them.

But soon there was just the sound of their song trailing behind as they paddled into the faraway.

Every spring when the ice had well and truly melted, the voyageurs set off from my home near Montreal in their beautiful honey-colored canoes. Where did they go? What did they do there? What did they carry away in those canoes? What did they bring back when they returned months later with the autumn wind at their backs?

Sometimes on their return I caught the scent of the faraway: Pinecones sticky with resin. The sweet sap of maple trees. Musky mushrooms. Juicy berries. A multitude of nuts and seeds yet to be tasted.

It was a smell that stirred up in me a wander-lust—a call to adventure of the grandest sort.

"I want to be a voyageur," I told my friends.

"Why?" they asked.

"They are brave. *I* am brave!

"They are strong. *I* am strong!

"They like to sing. *I* like to sing!

"They carry heavy bundles. I carry . . . things.

"They wear red caps and sashes. I wear red from head to tail!

"The voyageurs are small in stature," I said. "*I* am small! Why should I not be a voyageur?"

"Because you are a squirrel?" my friends argued.

"Because you cannot paddle a canoe?"

"Because you cannot cook?"

"Because, at the portages, you cannot carry a heavy bundle?"

This is what I said to them: "I may not paddle, but I can sing! I may not cook, but I can eat! I may not carry much, but I can carry *something*!"

"Well," said my friends, "they will never let you into their canoe."

"Perhaps," I agreed. "But their canoes are so big there are plenty of places to hide. And I am so small I can fit into one of their vest pockets."

MY JOURNEY BEGINS

And that is exactly where I was when the next brigade set off. *Oui, c'est vrai!* Yes, it's true! I joined a crew of eight hearty voyageurs:

Jean Méchant

Jean Paul

Jean Luc

Jean Jacques

Jean Henri

Jean Claude

Jean Louis

Jean Gentille

Et moi, Jean Pierre Petit Le Rouge, the littlest voyageur.

Jean Méchant

Jean Paul

Jean Luc

Jean Jacques

Jean Henri

Jean Claude

Jean Gentille

Jean Louis

The Jeans were not exactly *aware* that I had joined their team, but I planned to impress and delight them with my many talents.

As soon as I was in the canoe, I slipped out of the vest pocket where I had been hiding. I stashed myself among the kegs and barrels and oilcloths, and the many big, heavy canvas-wrapped bundles they call *pièces*.

But before the voyageurs departed, wives and sisters and mothers came down to the waterfront to say goodbye to their husbands, brothers, and sons. The clerks and gentlemen of the North West Company, the voyageurs' employers, came to wave farewell, too. Speeches were made, cannons fired, flags waved, songs sung. Finally the canoes were launched, and we were in the water!

Oh! The exhilarating *whoosh* of the canoe surging along under the power of eight strong paddlers! The speed of it was astounding! If I'd had a red cap to hold on to, I would have been holding on tight.

The five canoes in our brigade launched all at the same time, and every one wanted to be the fastest. Forty-some paddles flashed in the sun. Who would be first?

Not us. We were, in fact, last.

Perhaps with my encouragement, our canoe would soon be number one!

WE PADDLE UP THE OTTAWA RIVER

It wasn't long before I found myself, nose to the wind, perched on the bow of the canoe. The men dipped and swung their bright-bladed paddles while I called out "Strrrrrrroke!" Again and again, forty to sixty strokes per minute. "Strrrrrroke!"

The steersman, Jean Méchant, barked from his place in the back, "What a noisy chirring racket! Who brought that squirrel along? Was it you, Jean Paul?" He poked the middleman sitting in front of him.

"*Mais non*," Jean Paul said, then nudged the middleman who sat next to him. "Perhaps it was Jean Luc."

"Not me," said Jean Luc. "Were we *supposed* to bring squirrels?"

"No!" everyone shouted at him.

Like me, Jean Luc was making his first trip as a voyageur. He couldn't be expected to know everything!

"Maybe it was Jean Henri," Jean Luc said, tapping the middleman in front of him with his paddle.

"Not me," said middleman Jean Henri.

And so they went, along all three rows of middlemen:

It was not middleman Jean Jacques.

Not middleman Jean Claude.

Not Jean Louis, also a middleman.

Not even the bowman, Jean Gentille, who sat in the very front of the canoe to guide it. Unbeknownst to him, it was in *his* vest pocket that I had hidden.

From my perch on the bow, I tried to explain my goals and aspirations. "My name is Jean Pierre Petit Le Rouge, and I am an adventurer. I long to explore the unexplored, discover the undiscovered, and taste the as yet untasted."

"I hope he won't be a nuisance," said Jean Méchant from the back of the canoe.

"He's only a squirrel," said Jean Gentille.

I vowed to not be a nuisance. No, I certainly intended not to be, for what joy it was to feel the wind in my fur, to see the playful otters swimming by and the bright rings made by jumping fish. What a thrill to hear the slap of the beaver's tail and the wild call of the loon. And what heaven to smell the spring blossoms and sun-warmed pine.

And oh, how I loved to sing!

The voyageurs also loved to sing.

"En roulant, ma boule roulant," Jean Jacques, *le chanteur* (the singer) started us off.

"En roulant ma boule," the others joined in.

They did their best, but this song about getting a ball rolling could be a bit repetitive. I tried to encourage them to put in a little flourish.

"En rrrrr-rrrrrr-rrrrrrrrrroulant, ma boule rrrrr-rrrrrrroulant!" I sang out. (Even the Frenchest of Frenchmen cannot roll his *r*'s like me. I can keep it up all day if I have to. Or even if I don't.)

I scampered along the gunwale, encouraging each man to sing with more gusto. Perhaps this would make us go faster and we could overtake the other canoes in our brigade. This was my thinking, but the others didn't seem to agree.

Some of the voyageurs covered their ears; others began swinging their paddles at me.

"That's enough of that noise!" Jean Jacques yelped.

"Shoo!" said Jean Paul. He swatted at me with his cap.

"*Va-t'en!*" Jean Claude swiped at me with his paddle. "Go away!"

It was a wonder the entire canoe did not tip upside down.

And then I saw Jean Gentille motioning to his vest pocket. "*Chut,*" he whispered. "Hush! Jump inside!"

I did. And there I crouched, panting.

"Where did the little pest go?" Jean Jacques asked.

"I don't care, as long as he's gone," I heard Jean Méchant say.

"What do we do now?" Jean Luc said.

"Paddle!" Jean Méchant barked. "And put your backs into it!"

"But," Jean Claude asked, "where are the other canoes?"

The voices grew concerned.

"Are we lost?" they wondered.

"We were so busy with that pesky squirrel that we have gotten separated from our brigade!" Jean Paul said.

The part of the Ottawa River where we were paddling was a maze of islands and peninsulas, bays and inlets. It would take hours of paddling to find the others. If we could.

"Now what shall we do?" Jean Luc cried.

The voyageurs pulled the canoe to the shore and they all jumped out.

"It is the fault of that chattering rascal," said Jean Méchant.

The others grumbled their agreement.

"If he hadn't distracted us, we would still be following the others," said Jean Jacques.

Sacrebleu! Oh, no! I thought. It was true. It was my fault. I wanted to set it right. But alas, what could I do? I, who was so small and insignificant?

But then I had an idea. I thought, *I may not paddle. I may not cook. When we get to a portage, I may not carry much. But there is something at which I am very, very good.*

I climbed out of Jean Gentille's pocket and quickly found the highest pine tree in the entire wilderness. Up I ran, as fast as I could.

Below me, the river split into many glittering waterways, divided by a confusion of islands and peninsulas. But—there! What did I see in the distance? The flash of paddles and four canoes laid out like a dotted line across a map.

I chirred! I trilled! I rolled my *r*'s with great ferrrrrrrrrocity!

The voyageurs looked up at me.

"Is that the same squirrel?" said Jean Méchant. "It sounds like the one that recently caused us so much grief."

Have I mentioned that sometimes these men were not very bright?

Ah, but Jean Gentille looked up at me with a smile on his face. He knew!

"Wait!" he said. "I think the little red one has

found our brigade. I think that is what he is chattering about."

"Found our brigade?" the others said. "How is that?"

"Why, he can see them, from his perch in the treetop."

Meanwhile, I was practically doing headstands up there—pointing with my paw, then my tail, then my entire body. When Jean Gentille whistled for me, down the tree I raced, over the boulders, up his trouser leg and onto his shoulder.

"Can you show us the way, little one?" said Jean Gentille.

"*Oui! Oui! Oui! Oui!*" I chirred, and "*Oui! Oui! Oui! Oui!*" again, in case they missed it the first time.

Jean Gentille said to me, "You shall ride on the bow of the canoe and show us the way."

"A squirrel? You are going to put your trust in a squirrel?" Jean Méchant said. "Ho ho! You are as nutty as he is!"

The others also seemed skeptical, but they

climbed back into the canoe. We set off, with me on the bow pointing the way with my nose. I cheered enthusiastically when they steered the right way, and scolded with all my might when they steered the wrong way.

Soon we saw the bright, flashing paddles of the other canoes. We had found our brigade.

"*Youpe!*" cried my canoe-mates. "Yippee! Hip, hip, hoorah!"

And I joined them, crying, "Hoorrrrrrrrah," leaning a bit heavily on the *r*'s, perhaps.

"Oh!" teased the voyageurs in the other canoes, when we caught up to them, "did the wittle boys get wost?" They threw back their heads and laughed.

"We always knew which way to go," said Jean Henri.

"We were never really lost," said Jean Claude.

"Good job, Le Rouge," Jean Gentille whispered to me, shortening my name a bit.

Did the others not know it was I who had shown them the way? I? Me? *Moi?* Jean Pierre Petit Le Rouge? *Jean Pierre Little the Red*, if you want a direct translation. Although perhaps *Jean Pierre the Little Red* is more musical. At least when it is spoken in French.

Ah well, what did I care? The wind ruffled my fur. And I sang. I sang at the top of my lungs! "*C'est moi*—it's me! Jean Pierre Petit Le Rouge of the Big Voice and *mon bon ami*—my best friend— Jean Gentille of the Big Heart."

OUR FIRST PORTAGE
STILL ON THE OTTAWA RIVER

For a time, I was a hero. It's true! A hero! Well, maybe not a hero, but at least I was tolerated. The voyageurs allowed me to stay in the canoe. Perhaps only in the bottom of the canoe—

"And no singing!" Jean Jacques grumbled, with a shake of his finger.

But even that status didn't last long.

I had been trying very hard not to irritate anyone—not singing, not running up and down the gunwales, not pestering anyone in any way. Instead, I stayed curled up in the bottom of the canoe, whiling away the time among the bundles of goods we carried.

It is, of course, difficult to be an explorer when

you can't see anything. How is one supposed to discover anything at all? Well, let it not be said that I am not resourceful. Indeed, after a day of this I realized I could explore right where I was. For instance, what was inside these parcels?

I decided to make a tiny hole in one of them to see what was in there. Just the *tiniest* hole. Then I would be able to press my eye against the itty-bitty hole and look inside.

And so I began to chew. I gnawed a very small hole, but as soon as the hole was made, *ping!* out popped a bead. A tiny white bead. And *ping ping ping*—red, yellow, blue—several more tiny beads. Then more. And more.

What to do?

I did the only thing I could think of: I crammed my paw into the hole to keep any more beads from popping out.

But, now, what did I smell? A whiff of something. A rather delicious smell coming from this other bundle. Convenient to my teeth. Soon my teeth had chewed a little hole in that one, and *click!* out came a little dried pea. *Tick click clatter tap*, a pawful of peas fell out. Oh, dear. I quickly stopped up the hole with my other paw.

Before I could think of what to do about the holes, the brigade came to a place where the waterway turned into roiling rapids. Roaring and growling and foaming, the river tumbled over rocks and boulders.

"Now what do we do?" Jean Luc asked.

"We must portage," said Jean Gentille. "That is when we carry the canoe and our cargo over land to where the water, she is calm again."

The voyageurs paddled to shore, jumped out of their canoes, and began unloading all the gear. It was a scene of such hustle and bustle as to make you want to turn a few somersaults just to fit in. I leapt out of the canoe, executed a few of those, and threw in a few flips for good measure.

But I had to scamper out of the way as Jean Claude dogtrotted by me carrying not one, but two *pièces* on his back, secured by a strap around his forehead.

After Jean Claude came Jean Jacques, then Jean Luc, and finally Jean Henri, who was carrying two heavy bundles *and* a keg on top! I trotted after them as they jogged down the portage trail.

But after a while it seemed that two of the loads were getting a little bit lighter. With each step, somebody was losing something.

A little trail of beads.

A little trail of peas.

"Jean Luc, you are so careless. Look what you have done," Jean Henri said.

"What have I done?" whimpered Jean Luc.

"Look at the ground," Jean Henri said.

Jean Luc saw the trail of beads. "I did nothing! It wasn't me! Anyway, your bundle is doing the same thing."

Jean Henri turned around to see a little trail of peas. He shrugged off his load and inspected the bundles. "Why, there are teeth marks here," he cried. "Tiny teeth marks! And a tiny hole. It looks as if a mouse or a squir—" He stopped himself mid-sentence, and glared at me.

I turned a darker shade of red.

"That little troublemaker!" Jean Henri shouted.

"After him!" the others cried. Throwing down their loads, they rushed at me.

You can be sure I disappeared up the first tree I saw. Up and up and up, until I reached the top. From there, I flung myself onto another tree and another, all the while proclaiming my innocence down at them. Well, not my innocence, but I tried to explain that I hadn't intended to cause any harm. But the voyageurs, they paid no attention.

Then here came the canoe, carried by Jean Méchant, Jean Gentille, Jean Louis, and Jean Paul. Only four men to carry that big canoe! Such is the miracle of birch bark. They set it down to take a rest and to see what the commotion was all about.

"Come down, Le Rouge!" Jean Gentille called up the tree. "No harm done. I shall stitch up the holes with my needle and thread."

I peeked through the branches at the kind Jean Gentille, and thought, *Let it never be said that I am a quitter.* So, as the voyageurs picked up the canoe and their cargo again, I quietly climbed

down the tree and followed at a respectful distance. Then, when no one was looking, I sneaked
into Jean Gentille's vest pocket.

And so I remained for the entire trip up the
Ottawa River and its many rapids.

At each new set of rapids, the guide of the
lead canoe would decide how it should be ne-
gotiated.

Sometimes we paddled *up* the rapids—a lot
of hard paddling (I assume).

Sometimes everybody hopped out except
Jean Gentille in the bow and Jean Méchant and
one other voyageur in the stern. These three used
long poles while the rest of the crew used a rope
to pull the canoe and all its cargo—carefully!
carefully!—up the churning river. Everybody
but me.

My job, as I saw it, was to avoid falling out of
Jean Gentille's pocket into the foaming water.

It was only when the rapids were too difficult
or too dangerous to negotiate that we would portage.

"I feel bad that I am not helping to carry

anything," I squeaked to Jean Gentille from his pocket, as he trotted down a portage trail. "But then, I am hardly anything to carry. Isn't that so, Jean Gentille?"

There was only a grunt for an answer.

SOME DIFFICULT TRUTHS ARE ENCOUNTERED

Of course this trip up the Ottawa River to where it joined the Mattawa River took many days. And the trip up the Mattawa River took many more days. Many of those days we were roused before dawn—sometimes well before dawn, perhaps three or four o'clock in the morning, maybe even two o'clock. I wouldn't know, I am a squirrel—do you think I tell time?

The reason we struck off so early? *La vieille*, she was calmer then. Who is *la vieille*? The old woman—which is what we called the wind.

Even more horrifying than rising in the middle of the night to paddle, we had to do it *without eating breakfast!* Some may consider this inhumane. I consider it insquir*rele*.

But there was paddling and portaging to be done before we could eat. And what was breakfast when we finally ate it three hours after our day had begun? The same thing we had for dinner, left to cook all night over the embers: a thick soup of split peas or dried corn and salt pork. Two times a day, breakfast and dinner.

Of lunch, we shall not speak. Because there wasn't any.

~

Every night, our brigade pitched camp on the shores of wherever we were. The older men knew the good spots from many previous trips.

The voyageurs unloaded the canoes, carrying all the cargo onto dry ground. They carried the canoes onto the beach and tipped them over to serve as shelter from rain, wind, and dew when they slept.

For protection from the black flies and mosquitoes, they applied to their skin a mix of bear fat and skunk urine. This also served as a repellant to me. I usually made a little nest well away from the aromatic crew.

But before sleep, there was much for each crew member to do.

Jean Henri went out and gathered firewood. He was so strong he could break up big branches with his bare hands.

Jean Jacques sang while he got a fire going.

Jean Paul dug out the cook pots and food from one of the parcels while Jean Louis mixed up flour and water to make bannock, a kind of fried bread.

Jean Méchant barked orders at Jean Luc and Jean Claude. "You two fix the leaks in the canoe."

"How do we do that?" Jean Luc asked.

Jean Méchant smacked his forehead with his hand. "Stitch up the cracks in the canoe with spruce roots," he said between his teeth, "and apply pitch to the seams."

Jean Gentille had his nose in a book, reading. He loved to read. He carried an extra bundle of his own stuffed with books. Only books! And every chance he got, he read. Philosophy. Poetry. Plays. He knew all manner of wonderful things, too, although the other voyageurs didn't seem to appreciate it.

WE ARE CAMPED AT TALON FALLS

My crew was camped with our brigade at Talon Falls and there was much merriment. The reason? Up until now, on first the Ottawa, then the Mattawa, we had been going—how shall I say?— uphill. Or that's how it must have felt to paddle against the current.

But here was where the water changed her mind and decided to go the other direction. Which happened to be the direction we were going. Instead of paddling *up* the river, our canoes would run right down it.

Jean Jacques was leading everyone in singing *"Youpe, youpe sur la rivière"* (Hooray, hooray on the river). Everyone but Jean Gentille, who, as usual, was absorbed in his reading.

Everyone was in such a fine mood that nobody seemed to mind that I had climbed out of Jean Gentille's pocket and helped myself to some pea soup.

"Did you know," Jean Gentille said, as Jean Louis was dishing up the supper, "there is a fellow named Isaac Newton who has a theory that there is a force on earth called 'gravity' and we are all subject to its laws?"

"That is why I like to be out here in the wilderness," Jean Méchant said, "where I am subject to no laws at all."

"It says in this book," Jean Gentille continued, "that gravity is most commonly experienced as the agent that gives weight to objects. Judging by the weight of the cargo we carry across the portages, I believe we are indeed subject to the law of this 'gravity.'"

"I repeat that out here in the wilderness I am not subject to the laws of any government or any gravity," Jean Méchant asserted again. "What do the rest of you say?"

"Well, I don't know. . . . ," Jean Luc said. "Those bundles are very heavy. Something must make them so."

"What makes them heavy is all the things inside," Jean Méchant said. "If you take the things out, then they are no longer heavy."

"That is true," the other voyageurs agreed.

"I agree with this Newton fellow," I chimed in. "For I have always wondered what causes objects to fall. Pinecones, for instance."

"Look at that little squirrel with soup on his whiskers," Jean Méchant muttered. "Chattering away about nothing."

Nothing? Clearly, he did not understand. Perhaps a demonstration would clarify. I scampered a short way up a pine tree and said, "If I pluck a cone off a tree and let go, what happens? Does it float? No! It falls!" I dropped the cone. It landed on Jean Jacques's head.

"Ouch!" he yelped, squinting up at me.

"Something must be pulling on the pinecone to make it fall." I demonstrated with another cone. This one landed with a *plop!* in Jean Luc's soup.

Jean Luc shook his fist at me.

"What is pulling on it?" I asked. "The earth! The earth's gravity is pulling on it! That is what gives things weight." I let another cone go. This one splatted with a *whack!* right into Jean Méchant's upturned face.

He leapt up, mad as a hornet. "What is the matter with that pest? Why is he still with us?"

The others crowded around.

"He rides, but he doesn't paddle!" said Jean Paul.

"He eats, but he doesn't cook!" said Jean Louis.

"At the portages has he ever carried anything? Is it possible that he, himself, has been carried?" asked Jean Henri, staring pointedly at Jean Gentille.

"He has a terrible singing voice," Jean Jacques said, then did a very bad imitation of me by simply trilling his tongue on the roof of his mouth. "*Rrr. Rrr. Rrr.*" Really, it sounded nothing like me.

"He has to go," Jean Méchant grumbled.

"*Mais non,*" Jean Gentille said. "He is a clever

fellow. And full of enthusiasm. He showed us the way when we were lost. He doesn't weigh much. If you are worried about what he eats, he can have a portion of *my* food."

Jean Gentille was the best friend any voyageur could ever have and I loved him with each of the eight ounces of my being.

THE BERRY PICKING IS GOOD ON LAKE NIPISSING

How might I be useful? I wondered.

I considered it while pacing along the gunwales, while aimlessly somersaulting around the canoe, while singing voyageur songs at the top of my lungs. And, while absentmindedly gnawing on a leather strap, I realized I had very good teeth. Twigs, bark, rope, leather . . . you name it, I could chew through it.

And then, feeling a little rumble in my tummy, I had another thought. I was good at finding seeds, nuts, and berries.

As soon as we made camp on Lake Nipissing, I went out and picked a lot of strawberries.

When I got back to the camp, what did I hear but . . .

"Jean Gentille," Jean Méchant said. "We have discussed this and have decided that the little red one will have to go."

"But!" I interrupted. "I have gone out and picked strawberries. *Voila!*" I proclaimed, holding out my paws full of . . . well, there *had* been strawberries in those paws. Perhaps all the berries had not made it back to camp. In fact, perhaps none of them had. It had been a lot of picking! I got very hungry doing all that work.

"The squirrel has not earned a place in the canoe," said Jean Jacques.

"He cannot be a voyageur if he doesn't do anything that a voyageur does," Jean Henri put in.

"Yes, he will have to go," said Jean Claude.

"I believe the best way for him to go is in a *ragoût*," finished Jean Louis.

"A *ragoût*?" I squeaked. "What is that?"

The others did not hear me. They were snorting with laughter.

Only Jean Gentille did not laugh. "A squirrel stew?" he said, and looked very, very sad.

~

That night, curled up in Jean Gentille's pocket, I could not sleep.

I heard the lonely wolves yip and wail.

I heard the loons singing their sad songs to each other, from lakes far apart.

And I heard the crew discussing my fate:

Jean Louis would chase me.

Jean Claude would grab me.

Jean Méchant would chop off—ah, me—my head!

They discussed how to divvy up my estate:

My fur coat would go to Jean Méchant to line his moccasins.

My meat would go to Jean Louis for stew.

My bones would go to Jean Luc for sewing needles, and my sinews to Jean Jacques for guitar strings.

Alas, I was not long for this world.

Perhaps I should run away. It would be a hard, sad, and lonely life for me. I had only ever wanted to be a voyageur. But what is a voyageur without paddling mates? What is a voyageur without a canoe?

How I would miss the feel of the wind in my fur! No longer would I see the bright rings the jumping fish made or hear the slap of the beaver's tail—at least not from the bow of a voyageur canoe.

Still, I could not ask my friend to protect me any longer.

I pondered all of this until we reached the French River where I made up my mind. I *would* run away.

THERE IS SOME DANGER
ON THE FRENCH RIVER

In the morning, while the voyageurs were loading the canoes, I tiptoed away from the camp.

I followed the shoreline until I came to a mossy bank that lined the swiftly flowing river. There I plunked myself on a rock, head in paws, to think about where I should go next. Should I go west on my own or should I try to make my way back to Montreal? I was terribly homesick!

Just then, I saw the brigade coming down the foaming river, wending their way around boulders in the rapids. One by one, the canoes went by.

Over the roar of the water, I heard the shouts

of the voyageurs. Were they calling me to come back and jump into the stewpot? Ho ho! That was not going to happen!

But, *sacrebleu!* The last canoe was upside down! *My* canoe! Red caps bobbed up and down as the voyageurs were swept downstream. There they went:

Jean Paul . . .

Jean Luc . . .

Jean Henri . . .

Jean Jacques . . .

Jean Louis . . .

Jean Claude . . .

Jean Méchant . . .

Mon Dieu! My friends were in danger. And where was Jean Gentille? What if . . . I dared not think of it!

There he was, swirling and spinning, twisting and twirling in the foamy river. Then—oh, no!— he disappeared under the water!

I bounded up and over fallen logs, along branches, as fast as I could go, trying to catch up to Jean Gentille.

His head popped up, and oh my! He'd lost his cap and his head was as hairless as a baby bird. I leapt out onto a boulder in the river.

"Grab my tail!" I chirred.

But before he could reach me, Jean Gentille was swept under again. Down the river he rushed, bobbing up and down in the current.

I flitted and flew through the cedars. Just as Jean Gentille's head came up again, I scampered out on an overhanging bough.

"Take my paw!" I squeaked, but once again he disappeared under the water.

Where was he? Where was my friend? I waited. I watched. I trembled.

The other canoes of our brigade had stopped and the men were snagging our gear and parcels out of the water, along with my voyageurs and our canoe. My wet crew sat on the shore in their soggy shirts and dragging sashes and dripping beards. Some of the others had lost their caps in the river too.

The other men started to lay out our wet cargo to dry. In addition to the food we had to carry for ourselves—split peas, dried corn, and salt pork—there were wool blankets and bolts of scarlet cloth, mirrors, cooking pots and utensils, silver earbobs and trinkets, twists of tobacco, bags of flour, and things that made my fur stand on end: axes and knives, guns and ammunition, and most sinister of all . . . animal traps.

What do they do with all of these things? Especially those (shudder) traps?

I couldn't wonder for long, for there! Sitting by the side of the river without his cap! Jean Gentille, shivering and wet, rubbing his hands together, his teeth chattering. He must have been very cold, especially with his head so bald and bare.

But there was a red cap, swirling along in the water, drifting close to shore. Jean Gentille reached down to snag it but another hand snatched it up before he could get to it. It was Jean Méchant! He wrung the hat out and plunked it on his own head.

Perhaps there was one small thing I could do to help Jean Gentille. Even though I knew that at any moment I might be grabbed and thrown into the stewpot, if there was something I could do for him, I wanted to do it.

I climbed up his pant leg and from there up his sleeve onto his shoulder. And from his shoulder onto his head. There I tenderly curled myself into a hat. I would be the warmest of warm fur hats for my cold friend.

From then on, down all the rapids of the French

River, and along the northern channel of Lake Huron, many days' worth of travel, I rode proudly upon Jean Gentille's head. The others all agreed that Jean Gentille's poor bald head needed a hat, so there I stayed. On sunny days I shielded him from the sun. I protected his head from rain and sleet. On windy days I clung tight, and I vowed that when the cold snows came I would keep his ears warm. I'd be his hat for as long as he liked, for we were the best of friends.

ON TO LAKE SUPERIOR

After a long portage around some very big, terrifying rapids, the full joy of the voyageur's life was revealed to me.

At last we were on big, beautiful, and dangerous Lake Superior.

We traveled swiftly in our birch-bark canoe.

She glided through the water without a sound.

She wove around rocks as if she knew the way.

She kept us dry on rainy nights.

Some days the wind howled out of the north, cold and bitter. There were cool days and days of driving rain. On warm days the air was fragrant with pine. There were days of fog and days of dazzling sunlight.

They were all good days.

THERE IS FOG

One morning the fog on the lake was as thick as Jean Louis's pea soup. And for a change our canoe was first in the brigade. The other canoes paddled in a line, each bow close to the stern of the canoe ahead. It was up to Jean Gentille to navigate the entire brigade through the fog— to keep us from running aground, or smashing into cliffs or submerged rocks.

But how?

The voyageurs, poor humans that they are, possess a sadly underdeveloped sense of smell. They don't hear so well, either. *Moi?* My hearing is excellent and my sense of smell is so well tuned, I can find pine seeds under three feet of snow. This was a job for me!

I abandoned my post on the top of Jean Gentille's head and climbed onto the bow to put my ears to work. I would scold, scold, scold if I heard waves splashing against the shore, or the sploosh of a turtle sliding off a rock. That meant we were too close to danger.

At the same time, I held my nose high, twitching with the effort of smelling all that needed to be smelled: Blossoming chokecherry trees and peppery lupines, a chickadee nest in a birch tree. Deep in the woods in a north-facing depression, an old patch of snow, as yet unmelted. *Otters have been here*, I thought. *Steer clear!* Otters are not to be trusted. A mink has made a little den among some roots along the shore. Nothing smells as smelly as a mink. Unless it's an otter.

"We are too close to shore!" I barked. "Steer away!"

Jean Gentille directed Jean Méchant to steer away.

At last the fog began to clear. Just in time, for

I was exhausted by my efforts. So fatigued was I that I tumbled off the bow right into the lake!

My crew just laughed as I sputtered and gasped. That water was cold!

But kind Jean Gentille scooped me up with his paddle and set me inside the canoe.

I shook myself dry and climbed back onto his head.

WE ENCOUNTER *LA VIEILLE*

No sooner had the fog lifted than the old woman, the wind, picked up. She blew so wildly, she pushed the water into huge, fierce waves that splashed into the canoes and threatened to sink us all.

The brigade was *dégradé*—forced ashore by wind and waves. One by one the canoes entered the shelter of a small cove, where the voyageurs disembarked.

Jean Louis went off to hunt seagull eggs.

Jean Henri moved some boulders around, just for the fun of it.

Jean Gentille, of course, pulled out a book.

Across the lake, along the horizon, lightning made jagged streaks against the sky. A few moments later, thunder roared.

Jean Gentille looked up from his book and said, "Did you know that light has a finite speed? It doesn't travel instantaneously as we have always assumed."

"I never thought any such thing!" Jean Luc said.

"That's because you've never thought *anything*!" Jean Méchant laughed.

"It says in this book that sound also has a finite speed," Jean Gentille went on, "slower than light."

Lightning flashed, closer now. A moment later, the deafening roar of thunder.

"Perhaps that explains why one sees the lightning first, and afterwards hears the thunder," I said, pointing my tail in the direction of the storm, then covering my ears with my paws.

Jean Gentille looked at me. "I wonder . . . ," he said. "I don't know why, but Le Rouge has made me have a thought."

"Again with the thoughts!" the others groaned.

"Perhaps that is why we see the lightning first, and afterwards hear the thunder," Jean Gentille said.

I beamed. My fur glowed an incandescent shade of orange.

"Perhaps what the lightning and thunder is trying to tell us is that we are about to get very wet!" cried Jean Luc.

Everyone leapt up and raced around scooping up the gear. Then it—and they—all went under the canoes while the heavens opened and the rain poured down. As for me, I found a hole in a tree where I could curl up nice and dry.

SPIFFING UP AT HAT POINT, LAKE SUPERIOR

We had been traveling for many weeks when the others began to speak of "the Great Rendezvous." From what I gathered, this was a very important event—a big party waiting for us at our destination: the trading post at Grand Portage on Lake Superior. I learned that all the many goods we'd carried with us would be traded for other things. I couldn't wait to find out what the other things would be!

Before we got to Grand Portage, the brigade stopped at Hat Point to clean the canoe and spiff themselves up. Some men trimmed their beards, some scrubbed the soot from their fingernails, and they all rubbed bear fat into their hair so it glistened. They put on their best shirts and brightest sashes and tucked big feathers in their caps.

While they were spiffing themselves up, I did the same. I gave my coat a good going-over, picking out all the nits and gnats.

Finally, with shining faces and glistening hair (and fur), we set off for Grand Portage.

PART II

THE GREAT RENDEZVOUS

GRAND PORTAGE

My heart was thrumming as we rounded the point and beheld the stockade that surrounded the trading post. From my place on top of Jean Gentille's head, I saw buildings inside the stockade and many tents outside.

The long sand beach was lined with dozens and dozens of canoes belonging to the brigades that had arrived before us.

On shore, voyageurs were carrying gear, mending canoes, chopping wood, and tending campfires. Such a swirl of people!

Soon our canoes joined those of other brigades on the beach and we began unloading our cargo. And by "we" I mean the other Jeans.

"What do we do with our goods?" Jean Luc asked.

"We carry all our cargo to one of the warehouses inside the trading post," said Jean Gentille, "where everything will be unpacked, sorted, repacked, and weighed."

"So then we pick up what we came for and go home?" Jean Luc asked.

"No," growled Jean Méchant. "First we work."

"Work?" Jean Luc squeaked.

"Work," the others all echoed.

"We portage bundles, bales, and kegs over the *grand portage* to Fort Charlotte," said Jean Paul.

"And portage other bundles and bales back," added Jean Jacques.

"It's only seventeen miles round trip," Jean Henri casually mentioned.

"Then we do it all again," said Jean Paul.

"Several times!" Jean Henri added enthusiastically.

"When we're done with that we do whatever else the bosses here tell us to do."

"Cut firewood."

"Repair buildings."

"Repack items."

"And so on," said Jean Claude.

"Six days of work . . . ," said Jean Paul.

"Oh," Jean Luc said, sounding disappointed.

"Then six days of fun!" Jean Paul finished.

"Singing!" sang out Jean Jacques.

"Eating!" Jean Louis smacked his lips.

"Tests of strength!" Jean Henri bellowed.

"Fighting!" Jean Méchant growled.

"And reading," Jean Gentille said with a happy sigh.

SIX DAYS OF WORK

While my crew was portaging, sawing up fire-wood, hammering nails, and doing whatever the bosses told them to do, I left Jean Gentille hatless and went exploring.

First I visited the camp of the northmen, who came from farther inland. When my brigade traveled back to Montreal, the northmen would paddle the other direction—west and north—on the smaller waterways, to ever more remote trading posts. There they would spend the winter. They were hardy fellows, and braggarts. For reasons that escaped me, they didn't have to do any work when they got to Grand Portage. They lounged around and made fun of the *mangeurs du lard*, the pork eaters, which is what they called us. As if we were spoiled schoolboys!

I visited the nearby village of the Anishinaabeg, too. The smoke from their campfires smelled deliciously of wild rice, smoked fish, and sweet maple. Their smaller canoes lined the beach—light, strong, waterproof, and beautiful. The Anishinaabeg were the inventors of the wonderful craft that had carried us and our cargo over a thousand miles so far.

And finally I snuck into the stockade, hoping to find out what we were going to get for our trade goods. I visited a blacksmith's, a cooper's, and a carpentry shop, and I managed to get inside the mess house where the clerks and partners of the North West Company took their meals.

These gentlemen in top hats and tailcoats were the bosses who ran the whole operation, and they ate well! Their table groaned with platters of roast pork and smoked fish, kettles of venison stew and bowls full of fresh vegetables.

Personally, I think they overreacted when

I only wanted a small taste of a few of these things—I suddenly found myself outside, swept there by a broom-wielding cook.

And I did not discover a single thing about what we would receive in exchange for our trade goods.

SIX DAYS OF FUN

When the work was done, my crew joined in the festivities outside the stockade. All day and all night, the voyageurs feasted; they danced; they bragged; they fought.

Fists flew. Scrapes, scratches, big black eyes. Broken teeth. And noses, also broken, sometimes for the fourth or fifth time.

Did I mention before that these men were not always so smart? Brave? Oh, yes, very brave! Strong? My, yes, very strong. Smart? Sadly, not very smart.

The only one who didn't have a broken nose was Jean Gentille. That was because he kept his nose in a book. Reading by firelight at night, and daylight by day.

One morning he was reciting to me from plays by an Englishman named Shakespeare. "*To be or not to be*," he began.

What kind of question is that? I wondered. Either you are or you are not, is that or is that not so? Also, who wanted to philosophize when we had yet to find out what we would be getting in exchange for our goods? I was so anxious to find out that I had a hard time staying still.

"What is wrong with you, Le Rouge?" Jean Gentille asked.

"What is wrong with me? What is wrong with me is curiosity!" I squeaked and chattered. "We have traveled all this way, weeks and weeks we have been paddling—well, *you* have been paddling—and over many grueling portages. (I *assume* they were grueling.) These goods we (you) have carried all this long way I know are meant to be traded, but traded for what? For what? For what? For what?"

"Ohhhh," groaned Jean Paul, who had been asleep nearby. "Can you make him stop that noise? My head hurts."

His head hurt from staying up well past his bedtime, not because of my chattering. I wanted to explain that to him, but by now I realized that these men either could not or *would* not understand me.

A HORRIBLE DISCOVERY IS MADE

"*Allons-y!*" shouted Jean Méchant. "Everybody from our canoe, let's go!"

"What are we doing?" asked Jean Luc.

"It is time to prepare our goods for the trip back to Montreal. We leave tomorrow."

This was it! The big moment. I couldn't help but squirm with anticipation.

"Le Rouge," Jean Gentille scolded, "all this crawling about on my head is making my scalp itch!"

"*Pardonnez-moi,*" said I jumping off. "Excuse me, but I am excited!"

And why was I excited?

Because, at long last, I would find out what we would receive in exchange for our goods.

It made me want to sing!

I trembled with excitement as I scampered up the trail.

I could not help a few acrobatics on the way.

I chirped!

I barked!

I threw in a few somersaults.

We came to a building.

"Is this it?" Jean Luc asked.

"This is it," Jean Méchant said.

"This is it!" I squeaked, and when the door opened, I flew inside ahead of the others. What would I find? Buckets of pine seeds? Piles of acorns? Boxes of mushrooms?

But I saw none of these things. Instead, what did I behold?

The skins of dead animals.

To the front of me.

To the back of me.

To each side of me.

And even above me.

The skins of wolves, martens, bears, lynxes, raccoons, minks, and beavers hung from the rafters. Especially beavers. Beaver pelt after beaver pelt. Dozens—no, hundreds—of pelts, furs, skins.

And traps. Dozens of metal traps. Traps that shut with a sickening snap! A splintering crunch!

What could it all mean?

We had come such a long way for *this*?

Perhaps some horrible mistake had been made, I thought. But, no! I saw the man behind the counter counting out skins.

"What is this place?" Jean Luc asked, looking around at the furs and all the other trade goods.

"This is the trade store," said Jean Méchant.

The rafters were hung with pelts, and furs were stacked on tables. Shelves were piled high with blankets, bolts of cloth, beads, and silver jewelry. There were birch-bark boxes and baskets full of wild rice and maple sugar.

"Here the Anishinaabeg come to trade, bringing furs, fish, game, wild rice, and maple sugar, and here we pick up our furs for the return trip," explained Jean Gentille. "These furs will be packed into bales, weighed, and bundled up for the long voyage to Montreal and beyond."

"B-B-B-But . . . ," I stammered. I ran along the shelves to talk to them. *Perhaps* I knocked a few beads off as I went. I *might* have spilled a little wild rice. *Maybe* a few silver trinkets clattered to the floor.

But was that any reason to chase me?

Around and around the store I went, with several voyageurs close behind. I scampered up into the rafters.

"Shoo! Shoo!" the voyageurs said.

"Shoo! Shoo!" shouted the man behind the counter. "Or do you want us to hang your sleek red suit from the rafters, too?"

The men's laughter cut like daggers.

Off I went, a blur of red.

I darted.

I dashed.

I wove in and out of the furs.

Up and down the walls I went.

Here came the men after me. But it was a small space crammed with goods.

Jean Louis tripped.

Jean Paul slipped.

Jean Claude bumped into Jean Méchant.

Jean Méchant bumped into Jean Jacques.

Jean Jacques bumped into Jean Luc.

Jean Luc bumped into a big pile of cast-iron cooking pots that all tumbled down with a crash and a clatter.

Just as Jean Henri was about to snatch me by the tail, Jean Gentille scooped me up and carried me outside.

"Lucky for you," he said, "that you are not a beaver. For, you know, the Englishmen must have their hats. The hats made from the fur of beavers are so popular in England and Europe that every fellow there must have one or two or three."

I groaned.

"Also lucky for you that you are so small, Le Rouge," he said to me. "Your pelt is not very valuable. Otherwise, they would be more serious about trying to catch you."

At that I had to sit down with my head between my knees.

LATER THAT NIGHT

Outside the stockade, dozens of campfires lit up the night. Someone produced a fiddle. There was another fellow who played the fife. The voyageurs sang, and in the flickering light of the fires, the dancing began again.

As for me, I could not enjoy the party. Even though I am red, I was—how do you say?—blue. What was I doing here, so far from home? How I longed to be in my own little nest in the treetop over the Ottawa River. How I longed to see my friends. But the only way to get home was with the voyageurs, and I could not go with them knowing what I knew now.

I made up my mind about what I must do. Into my handkerchief—okay, it was a part of Jean Gentille's pocket that I had gnawed out of boredom—I placed all my belongings:

an acorn

a small, perfect pebble

a tiny shell

a crumb of bannock, given to me by Jean Gentille and a pawful of pine seeds.

"I am going into the woods," I chirred to my crew, "to live deliberately."

They didn't seem to be paying any attention to me.

"I will go confidently in the direction of my dreams," I continued. "I shall let my whiskers grow long and leave my fur ungroomed. I want to live deep and climb high, to see far, to suck the sap from the tree of life. Or, short of that, the tree of maple. Don't try to stop me!" I told them, holding up my paw. "I've made up my mind."

None of them seemed like they planned to try to stop me. Only Jean Gentille looked up from his book.

"If this is what it means to be a voyageur, I cannot be one," I told him, flinging my paw to my forehead. "To profit from the skins of my animal brethren—it goes against every fiber of my being, every bit of fluff in my undercoat, every guard hair, every whisker."

"My friend," I said, choking a little and staggering toward him, "I have always thought you to be a man of high ideals. It does not surprise me so much that these other voyageurs would engage in such brutality—they are cretins. But you—you are kind, noble, and educated. I would have expected more of you."

"You don't seem quite right, little one," Jean Gentille said gently. "Are you sick?"

"I am sick at heart," I said, then turned and trudged away, bundle in hand.

IN THE FOREST

My paws were silent on the mossy ground.

The trees were like black ribbons against a black dress. Everything dark.

A distant hoot, perhaps an owl.

Creaking branches.

Frogs, chirruping in a swamp. As I passed by, they instantly hushed. Then, not a sound.

A step.

Crunch.

Another step.

Crack.

Was I making that sound? Or was someone following me? *Maybe I should turn back*, I thought.

Perhaps Jean Gentille was pacing back and forth, fretting over me. "What has happened to my Le Rouge?" he might be saying.

The thought of this made me want to weep. Alas, my hanky was in use, with all my belongings tied up inside of it.

So preoccupied with these thoughts was I that I hardly noticed the ominous swish of large wings overhead. The large wings came swooping down toward me. Wings belonging to an owl!

"You must fly!" sang a voice—a feminine voice that did not belong to those large wings.

"Fly?" I said. "But I am a squirrel, and squirrels do not fly."

"Oh, do they not?" the voice said. And here came a squirrel flying—yes, flying!—straight toward me from the other direction. "If you cannot fly," said the soaring squirrel, "you'd better r—"

Her words were cut off by the loud beating of wings. A dark shadow covered me. A shadow that grabbed me with its sharp talons and lifted me up . . . up . . . up into the air.

"Fight for your life!" yelled the airborne squirrel.

I did! I did! Oh, how I struggled and fought and kicked and flailed, my bundle of worldly goods falling away.

But nothing I did loosened the grip of those wicked talons on my hide.

Up, up, up I went, toward the bright stars. But what was that? A pair of eyes glistened in the branches of a pine tree.

And a tiny voice proclaimed, "Here I come!" The creature launched herself into the sky again.

"*No, mademoiselle!*" I shouted. "*It's too far!*"

But the fragile beast stretched out her cape and soared, drawing ever closer to me.

The owl gave his wings one powerful beat, and surged ahead.

My heart sank as my rescuer sailed past.

But then—*snap!*—her tiny paws grasped my tiny toes.

We soared through the air with the greatest of ease. . . .

But only for a moment, so sorry to say, and

then the owl, apparently tiring, let go. With a sickening lurch of my stomach, I realized we two tiny creatures were falling . . . falling . . . (probably the fault of gravity) . . . falling . . .

WE ARE SAFE

A cozy little round room. That is where I found myself. A cozy little round room inside a tree. A sweet, piney-smelling tree.

My rescuer looked at me with enormous brown eyes set in a tiny little face.

"*Mademoiselle!*" I said, as soon as I regained consciousness and had taken in my surroundings. "I must thank you for saving me."

"My name is Monique," she said, "and you are . . ."

"My name is Jean Pierre Petit Le Rouge, and I am a voy—" I stopped. I was no longer a voyageur, I remembered.

"Were you going to say you are a voyageur?" she asked.

I shook my head. "I thought I wanted to be one, but . . . now that I know what kind of work they do, I don't think I can."

"Ah, you are a squirrel of ideals," she said. "I like that."

I'll admit it. That made me blush a darker shade of red.

"Please," Monique said. "You have had a most trying experience. You must be famished! Please have something to eat." She gestured to a repast of tiny wild strawberries, plump red thimble berries, bits of bark sticky with sweet sap, glowing orange chanterelles, sponge-like morels, and tidy piles of pine seeds.

"At last!" I exclaimed. "Real food!"

I tucked in. I tried some of everything—maybe all at once. After some moments, I realized I had perhaps been quite rude.

"Pardon me," I said, covering my mouth, which I'm afraid was rather full. "Is it your cape that allows you to soar through the air like that?"

"It is not a cape," said she. "It is my skin."

She demonstrated how her skin stretched between her front and hind paws, giving it a cape-like appearance.

"I am a flying squirrel," she explained.

"I am in your debt for saving my life." I gave a low bow and kissed her dainty paw.

"*C'est rien*," she said. "It is nothing. We are lucky that we landed in the soft branches of a fir tree, otherwise things might have ended very differently."

"This day has been a dangerous one," I agreed. "If not owls, then it has been men chasing me." I shuddered, remembering the incident at the trade store.

"Men!" Monique spat. "Ugh!"

"They're not *all* bad," I ventured to say.

"Thickheaded!"

"Well, yes. . . ." I had to agree.

"Vain!"

"Yes, that, too." I sighed. "But they are very brave."

"If you say so." Monique shrugged. "But really,"

said she, "I pity them. They are not good at climbing trees."

"They are not fast at running," I added.

"Their balance is very bad," she said.

"I have never seen one that could leap from one treetop to the next."

"Men are so ill-suited to life on this earth," Monique said, shaking her head. "They can't even keep themselves warm, except by stealing other creatures' skins."

"I believe the voyageurs are . . . misguided," I told her.

"If you say so," Monique said, offering me some more pine seeds.

"Perhaps there is a way of showing them the error of their ways," I suggested.

"I doubt it," Monique said.

"But if there *was* a way," I said, my mind whirring, "wouldn't it be worth a try?"

"What are you suggesting?" Monique asked.

"I will have to think about it," I told her, "even though thinking makes me uncomfortable. You see, I am a squirrel of *action*!"

"Of course," said Monique. "But action without thought is folly."

"I have thought about it now," I said.

"Already!" Monique exclaimed. "You are a fast thinker."

"Indeed I am, *mademoiselle*. And this is my thought: If the voyageurs really got to know the animals, they wouldn't want to take their pelts. They would see that each creature has their own personality, own uniqueness—and each has a great need for their own skin."

"But how would that ever happen?" Monique asked.

"What about a rendezvous with the animals?" I said. "There is nothing the voyageurs love more than a rendezvous. Singing! Dancing! Fighting! Well, maybe we will try to leave the fighting out of it. I, Jean Pierre Petit Le Rouge, will arrange it all."

I RALLY THE FUR-BEARERS

Thanks to my robust voice, it was not difficult to contact the animals—nocturnal or not—and invite them to gather for a *tête-à-tête*—a conversation, as it were—just before dawn the next morning. They were a little skeptical, but nearly all the invited guests arrived. Monique and I situated ourselves on a branch, keeping well above the heads of the predators. From there, I got their attention with a hearty cheer, or, as some call it, "chirr."

"Gentle creatures of the forest . . . ," I began. (Truth to tell, some of them are not all that gentle, but it's always best to be polite.) I went on to explain my idea in terms simple enough for even a chipmunk to follow, and ended with

"We must approach the voyageurs with our concerns."

Fox scoffed.

Bear guffawed.

Skunk laughed so hard that he let loose a little of his . . . er . . . perfume.

"How do you propose to converse with men?" Marten asked. "We understand many, many languages—we understand the crow's caw; we know the cries of the loon. And even your incessant prattle."

Prattle! I was about to protest when Monique laid a gentle paw upon my foreleg, reminding me to ignore any rude comments. Instead, I listened politely while Marten finished what he had to say.

"But these . . . these *Takers*," he went on, "they do not understand our languages. Not even the simplest."

One of the Raccoon twins picked up where Marten left off. "We have always lived in harmony with the First People, those who have lived here since the dawn of our time.

Before these Takers came, the First People took only what they needed. Every creature on earth must eat and every creature must stay warm somehow. This is something we animals understand. But now the First People kill more and more and more, many more than they themselves need for food and clothing. Why? Because the Takers want more and more and more. The Takers take and take and take, and these skins go off in canoes to faraway places where the need is insatiable."

"What does 'insatiable' mean?" whispered Chipmunk.

"It means never enough," Wolf explained. "It's never enough for the Takers. They just keep taking—maybe until we are all gone!"

I began again. "All you say is true, and that is why we must explain to the voyageurs—"

I was interrupted by Fox. "Even if they could understand us, they will not listen to us," he said. "They do not even see us. They see only our fur."

"There's no reasoning with them," called Wolverine.

"Fight! We must fight!" Mink shouted.

"Tear them to pieces!"

"Tooth and nail!"

"Claw and fang!"

"They will only get their shooting mechanisms and blow us all to smithereens," said solemn Badger.

"True," Monique said with a little sigh, and the others nodded.

"Man is a fickle creature," said Porcupine, who was in little danger of having his fur taken. "Today it's hats made of beaver fur; tomorrow it shall be—who can say? A hat made of feathers of birds, perhaps? Coats made of minks? Or a silly coat with tails, maybe. Ha ha! Wouldn't that be ridiculous?"

"Well, we fur-bearers must do our best to stay out of reach," Marten said as he and Fisher hustled away.

Wolf held her paw in the air. "I agree," she said, "it is best to avoid them—to stay as far away as possible."

Weasel and Snowshoe Hare said they planned to rely on their winter camouflage to stay safe.

"Of course I'm worried. This concerns me and my kind most of all, but I'm really too busy," Beaver said. "I've got a dam to repair and a house to build and . . ." He started to waddle into the underbrush.

The animals were all going away! I had to do something!

I chirred with such ferocity that my whole body quivered and my tail vibrated. "Whoever has not the stomach for it can go home now!" I cried, remembering a bit of a speech from a play Jean Gentille recently recited. "But stay, and you who outlive this day and see old age yearly on this day will say, 'Today is the day fur-bearers stood up for themselves.'"

I scampered up to a higher branch and called out, "And it shall never go by from this day to the ending of the world but we shall be remembered."

Up I went a few more branches. "We few, we happy few, we band of brothers and sisters," I called out. "For those that stand with me today shall be my brothers and sisters, even if she is (gulp) wolf. And all the other creatures who spent the day in their dens shall be sorry they were not here upon this day, which shall be known from this day forth and forever more as Fur-Bearers Day."

Not many animals can extemporize like this, but we red squirrels have a knack for it. There was a smattering of applause from those who had turned back to listen.

It had dawned a sunny day, and from my tree-top perch I noticed something. The voyageurs of my canoe were in the lake, scrubbing and singing, singing and scrubbing. Meanwhile, the other canoes of the brigade were being launched.

"Are you coming along?" the voyageurs in the canoes shouted to the men in the water.

"Yes, yes!" Jean Méchant called. "We will catch up!"

Their clothes and moccasins lay scattered all about on the beach. Their shirts and trousers hung from branches or were draped over rocks. And suddenly I had a plan.

THE PLAN IS EXECUTED

As the other canoes in the brigade began paddling away, the animals who decided to stay sneaked toward the shore.

Fox, Bear, and Wolf carried away trousers and moccasins.

Beaver, Skunk, and the Raccoon twins dragged away shirts and sashes.

The little ones, Mink and Weasel, stole caps and pouches.

Monique managed a scarf.

Even Chipmunk hauled away a sock.

Raven helped, too, just because he found it fun.

Finally the men scrambled out onto the beach.

"Hey! Who took my clothes?" Jean Louis said. "I left them right here."

"I blame the squirrel for this," Jean Méchant cried.

"No," said Jean Jacques. "On the portages he never carried a thing. He couldn't carry away all our clothes."

Jean Gentille smiled, and started to laugh. "Yes, I think this just might be his doing. That little one, he is clever. All right, Le Rouge, very funny! Bring back our clothes now."

But of course, there was no reply. All the animals, except for me, were sneaking away, the voyageurs' clothes in their teeth, paws and in the case of Raven, beak.

At first the other voyageurs laughed, too. Then they grew serious. Then cold. They began to shiver.

"We must go if we are to catch up with our brigade," said Jean Méchant.

"We cannot go paddling without any clothes!" Jean Paul protested. "The mosquitoes shall make a feast of us."

The other Jeans groaned.

"What do we do in this situation?" Jean Luc wanted to know.

"We don't know! We've never been in this situation!" the other voyageurs cried.

"I would like my trousers," said Jean Claude.

"Me too," said Jean Louis. "We can't go about like this. We will be laughingstocks!"

"I know where we can get something warm to cover ourselves," said Jean Henri.

"To the trade store!" cried Jean Jacques.

And, just as I thought they would, they all minced in their bare feet down the path. *Moi?* I raced ahead.

~

As soon as the voyageurs reached the store, they burst through the door. Since the clerk was not yet on duty, they just started snatching up pelts to cover themselves. A fox fur. A wolf pelt. A mink skin.

But suddenly Jean Paul yelped. "This fox pelt . . . ," he cried, "she is alive!"

"And also this mink!" wailed Jean Jacques.

"This bearskin rug is not a rug!" Jean Luc screamed.

"And this . . . oh, no . . . skunk! Aaahhhhh!"

"Eeeeeeee!"

"Iiiiiiiiiiiiii!"

"Ohhhhhh!"

Just then Jean Méchant caught a glimpse of me sitting in the rafters.

"You!" he shouted, while all the voyageurs ran screaming out of the store and into the woods.

We animals followed out the door, calling to them.

"Come back!" we yelled, running after them with the clothes we had stolen in our paws or teeth or beak.

"We didn't mean to frighten you," the gentle beaver called out.

But the men continued to run away.

"What is that smell?" Chipmunk asked.

"Me?" Skunk asked.

"No, that *other* smell," Chipmunk said.

We put our noses in the air and sniffed.

"Smoke!" Wolf said.

"Fire!" Mink cried.

"Oh no!' said Monique.

"Our campfire!" I heard Jean Jacques cry out. "We left it unattended!"

"As we know we should never do!" Jean Paul wailed.

The voyageurs raced toward their campsite while animals dropped the clothes and ran the other way.

Et moi? My instinct told me to run away, but my sense of duty insisted that I stay and help. I followed the voyageurs.

When we reached the site, we saw what had happened. The good news was that the wind had shifted and blown the fire toward the lake, where it burned itself out.

The bad news was that our beautiful canoe had been reduced to a pile of ashes. At least the cargo had been stowed well away from the canoe and remained undamaged.

There was a long, dark silence.

"*Mon Dieu,*" whispered Jean Méchant at last.

"What will we do?" cried Jean Jacques. "How will we ever catch up with our brigade?"

"How will we get home before the lakes freeze?" said Jean Henri.

"How will we get *home*?" Jean Luc wailed.

The Jeans found the clothes the animals had dropped and put them on. That made them feel better.

Jean Gentille had an idea. "Maybe we can borrow a canoe?" he suggested.

But the voyageurs in other brigades needed their canoes. Nobody had a spare.

"Maybe we can have a canoe made for us by the expert builders among the Anishinaabeg," said Jean Paul.

They went to the canoe builders and asked.

"Yes, we will build a canoe for you," said the head builder, "as soon as we finish the twenty orders ahead of yours."

The Jeans were despondent. They sat with heads in hands.

"We will never get home before the lakes freeze."

"We will have to stay here all winter."

"Our brigade will think we got lost."

"Our families will think, alas, we are no more. . . ."

"I am almost out of reading material," Jean Gentille said.

It was too much to bear. I wept.

Dragging my tail behind me, I returned to my animal friends who were waiting in the forest glen to hear what had happened.

"The fire is out," I told them.

They breathed a collective sigh of relief.

"But our beloved canoe has perished in the flames," I said. "Although I can no longer consider myself a voyageur, I will never stop loving that canoe. She glided through the water without a sound. She wove around rocks as if she knew the way. She kept us dry on rainy nights. And now there is no way for my crew to get home before freeze-up."

The animals looked downcast. None of us had wanted it to turn out this way.

"That is too bad," said Bear.

"We didn't mean for that to happen," Mink added.

"*Dommage!*" said Skunk. "Too bad!"

"Maybe there is something we can do," Chipmunk squeaked.

"I have watched the First People make their sleek canoes of birch bark," Raven said. "I know how it is done. We need the bark of birch trees, the wood of cedar, the root of spruce, the pitch of pines."

"If someone knows where there's a birch grove," Bear said, "I can gather a lot of bark."

Raven offered to show him the way.

Beaver said, "I could fell a cedar tree. We can use its boughs to make the thwarts and gunwales. It's not my favorite flavored wood, but if it would help to get them on their way . . ."

Skunk said he knew where there was a lot of *watap*—spruce root—"for the stitching."

"We're rather handy with our paws," the Raccoon twins put in. "If we can find Woodpecker and ask her to make the holes, we can do the lacing."

"I'll find Woodpecker," I volunteered.

"I can gather pitch from pine trees," Monique said.

"Let's get to work!" Raven cawed.

All the animals dispersed into the woods to tend to their chosen tasks.

THE CANOE, SHE IS FINISHED

We worked for the rest of the day and all night, and just before dawn we brought it to the campsite.

The voyageurs were sleeping.

Jean Gentille snored.

Jean Louis smacked his lips.

Jean Paul snorted.

Jean Jacques hummed.

Jean Henri groaned.

Jean Claude blew out little poofs of air.

Jean Luc clutched his blanket.

Jean Méchant was curled up like a baby, his thumb in his mouth.

We all carried the canoe into the campsite and left it there, a beautiful gift. There was a new paddle for each of them, too, personally gnawed by Beaver.

Then we tucked ourselves behind rocks and trees and watched. When the voyageurs awoke, what a surprise awaited them! A beautiful new canoe made of the bark of birch trees, stitched carefully with the roots of spruce trees, all the seams neatly caulked with the pitch of pines.

"But where did it come from?" Jean Gentille asked, looking all around.

"Who cares?" said Jean Jacques.

"Don't ask any questions!" said Jean Claude.

"Let's go!" the rest of them cried. "Not a moment to lose."

They quickly threw the cargo into the canoe, grabbed their paddles, jumped in, and shoved off.

The animals applauded and laughed.

I stood by, smiling.

Until, with a start, I realized something: "But wait! They cannot leave yet! Our mission has yet to be accomplished. We animals still haven't had our little *tête-à-tête.*"

"They don't want to discuss anything with us," Bear grumbled, popping a few ants into his mouth.

"But all of this—what was it worth," I cried, "if we cannot bring our concerns to them? No, I shall catch up with them and try to explain."

"I don't know if that's such a good idea. . . ." Monique said. "Anyway, look! They are already far away."

Paddles flashed in the distance. Wisps of a song trailed behind the canoe like mist.

I chirred, rolling my *r*'s as if my life depended on it.

They paid no attention.

I leapt.

I spun.

I did cartwheels, back flips, and a double backwards somersault.

They didn't look back.

Then I saw Monique running through the tops of the trees next to the shore. "Nutty squirrel," she called, "stop that foolishness and come with me!"

She dashed up into a large cedar tree that hung out over the lake. To the very tip-most twig of the farthest-reaching branch she went. Then she flung herself out, out, out, over the water. She soared and floated. Then, with a *plop*, she landed in the canoe.

My heart stopped beating. *"Mademoiselle!"* I squeaked.

The canoe was in an uproar. The pleasant singing had turned to angry curses, then shouts. Paddles swung and clashed as the voyageurs tried to scoop Monique out of the canoe. All the while, the boat rocked from side to side as Monique scampered along the gunwales, staying just out of the reach of angry hands.

By the time I rushed up the cedar tree to the very tip-most twig of the farthest-reaching branch, it was too late. The canoe was far out in the lake. I could not fly, like Monique. I could not swim. At least I would prefer not to. What could I do?

"*Sacre-bleu, mademoiselle!*" I cried. "What have I done? Those voyageurs—they are strong. They are brave. But they hate squirrels."

Then I had a happy thought. Eventually they would have to stop. When they did, Monique could leap out of the canoe and run away.

Then I had a sad thought. Monique might not survive until then.

But she was clever, no? She was fast. She would stay out of their reach, would she not? Perhaps Jean Gentille would take pity on her and protect her the way he protected me.

I would run along the lakeshore until I reached their campsite and be there when they disembarked. There I would find Monique and . . . and . . . well, we would cross that portage when we got to it.

LA VIEILLE SAVES THE DAY

As luck would have it, the old woman of the wind kicked up and forced the canoe ashore. Otherwise I am not sure I could have run long enough.

I hid in a tree and watched as the voyageurs climbed out, secured the canoe, and came to shore, one by one:

Jean Gentille

Jean Louis

Jean Claude

Jean Luc

Jean Jacques

Jean Henri

Jean Paul

Jean Méchant.

But what was this? Jean Méchant carried a bag that wiggled and moved.

I crept out on a branch over his head.

"This funny creature I have in this sack, I will take to Montreal," he said. "I will sell this animal to a circus. Imagine that—a squirrel trapeze artist!" Then, just as I was about to pounce on Jean Méchant, he said, "But if I ever get my hands on that *other* squirrel, that little red one—with him, I'll have Jean Louis make *ragoût*."

"Why wouldn't you sell *him* to the circus?" Jean Luc asked.

"The creature I have in this bag, well . . . she's got talent! But that other one, he is just an ordinary rodent. What could *he* do?"

"He had a loud voice," Jean Jacques said. Everyone laughed at that, as if it were a joke.

"He could eat a lot of pea soup," Jean Louis said.

Everyone laughed again. I didn't see what was so funny. A squirrel that works as hard as I do needs plenty of soup to keep him going.

"Remember how he wouldn't carry anything at the portages?" Jean Henri said. "In fact, it seems to me that he himself was carried!"

"And remember how he never paddled," Jean Claude said, "but he still liked to ride right in the front of the canoe?"

"Think of the mess he made at the trade store," Jean Paul said.

Listening to them, I began to feel very bad about myself.

Finally Jean Gentille spoke up. "Well, I don't know," he said. "I think he was rather a fine fellow. He was certainly the warmest hat I ever had."

"And you need a warm hat!" Jean Méchant joked, rubbing his hand on Jean Gentille's bald head.

"I liked his cheerful chirr," Jean Gentille said. "I liked his . . . enthusiasm. I rather miss the little fellow, and if he were to come back I would let him ride on my head again."

I melted with gratitude to hear Jean Gentille's kind words. I was so happy that I couldn't help it, I sang. I sang so robustly, I lost my balance. Out of the tree I tumbled, directly onto Jean Méchant.

WE ARE IN A PICKLE

We were in a pickle, Monique and I. She was tied up in a bag and I was, once again, held upside down by the tail over a stewpot by Jean Louis.

When Jean Gentille tried to intervene on my behalf, Jean Louis said, "You've saved the neck of this pest one too many times. It shall give me the greatest pleasure to see succulent portions of him swimming in my soup pot."

"Well, my dear," Monique said to me from the bag, "I'm glad you're here, but it is now or never. If there's something you want to say to these men, you should do it now or forever hold your peace."

Indeed, she was correct.

"Brave voyageurs," I began. In case you are unaware, it is not an easy thing to extemporize eloquently while being held upside down over a steaming stewpot. Still, I valiantly continued. "Please allow me to explain the extreme actions that were taken at the trade store. We didn't mean to frighten you. We just wanted to . . . discuss. To have a conversation. A *tête-à-tête*."

"Listen to him beg for his life, the rascal!" Jean Méchant said.

Beg for my life? I was doing no such thing. I was using my dying breath to try to save my fur-bearing brothers. "We fur-bearers wanted to talk with you about your involvement with the fur trade," I went on, perhaps a little too fast for their comprehension, but circumstances being what they were . . . "We understand that people need to eat and stay warm. We are predators ourselves, many of us. Ironically, though, not the beaver, whose fur you carry away in great quantities. He is a friendly fellow, welcoming to all, who eats nothing but leaves and twigs and bark—"

Jean Méchant interrupted me. "Is this squirrel going to be allowed to continue squeaking all day long?" he asked.

I squeaked more rapidly. "Yet he is being trapped into extinction." Knowing they had a hard time understanding me, I demonstrated. I pulled my own fur out by the pawful. "See? There is a limit. You can't keep taking and taking and expecting there to always be more."

"The little red one, he is making me think," Jean Gentille said.

"He is making me think, too," Jean Méchant said. "He is making me think about dinner."

"There is a lot of fur in the stewpot now," Jean Paul observed.

"No, but listen," Jean Gentille said. "We seem to take more and more beaver pelts back to Montreal every year. How many beavers do you think there are, anyway? Do you suppose it is possible to kill *all* of them, so there are none left?"

"No more beavers?" Jean Méchant said. "Oh, there are plenty of them, don't you worry about that! There will always be the beavers, the way there will always be the wolves, the caribou, the eagles, these big trees, this sparkling water. These things will always be here."

I have never claimed these men I traveled with were wise.

Strong? Yes.

Brave? Oh, my, very brave!

Tough? As tough as they come.

But wise? Sadly, no.

"If this is what you're getting from that chattering idiot," said Jean Claude, "tell the little squirrel that he doesn't need to worry about me. I've had enough. After this summer, I'm putting in for a desk job."

"I am going to France to become a chef," Jean Louis said.

"I am going to work on the railroad," said Jean Henri, flexing his muscles. "Just as soon as they start building one."

"I'm going to join a choir," said Jean Jacques, "and sing to my heart's content."

"I don't like the hours of this job," said Jean Luc. "I'm going to quit."

I was starting to feel very good about this, but then Jean Gentille said, "As for me, I am a voyageur and will be until I die."

My heart sank.

"Now let's make stew," said Jean Louis. "I shall drop the squirrel into the pot."

"But you must first remove the fur from the pot, *non?*" said Jean Paul.

"*Non*, that is where all the vitamins are," said Jean Louis.

There was a bit of a culinary disagreement, during which I found my wits. That is to say, I remembered that I have teeth. Sharp teeth. I twisted around and bit the hand that wanted to eat me.

Jean Louis jumped. His hand flew open and I flew out, landing on the ground.

I bolted straight up a tree. While Jean Louis leapt about, screaming, the other voyageurs stared up into the treetop, trying to spot me. They couldn't see me because I was dashing down the opposite side of the tree trunk. From there, I took a detour to the bag that imprisoned Monique, a bag tied shut with a leather lace. I took it in my teeth and bit down.

WHAT HAPPENS NEXT

Never had I chewed so hard or so fast in all my life.

A moment later, Monique was free—thank goodness for my needle-sharp teeth. We had only enough time to give each other a tender embrace, when—

"*Arrêtez*—Stop!" cried Jean Méchant. "Look there, the prisoner has escaped!"

All of the crew except Jean Gentille got up and scrambled after us. Their caps and sashes made streaks of red through the woods. They chased us around trees, over rocks, and through bramble bushes.

At last Monique and I scampered up a tree,

where they couldn't catch us. From there we could keep an eye on the crew, now a tangle of arms and legs.

"The wind, she has died!" Jean Gentille cried. "We must launch the canoes and try to catch up with our brigade!"

The others worked at untangling themselves while Monique and I caught our breath.

"That was a close call," Monique said. "Thank you for saving me."

"It was nothing," I said. "You are the brave one—throwing yourself into their canoe like that!"

"Perhaps that was not so smart," she said. "But, *monsieur*, what will you do now? You will have to go back with me. You can spend the winter. I have an extra room in my tree trunk."

I turned to Monique. "*Mademoiselle*," I said, "in spite of everything, I must go. Jean Gentille misses me. He is worried for me. And I worry for him. Without me to keep his head warm he might catch a bad cold. Also, I need to find some small treats for him—nuts and berries and so forth.

That is important because he never gets enough to eat."

"Why is that?"

"Because he gives his food to me."

"But maybe if you—" Monique began.

I had no time for arguments. *"Mademoiselle,"* said I, "never say that I am a quitter."

"I would never say that," she said. "But your crew have launched their canoe, and once again they are far away."

I looked. Indeed, she was right. I shook her paw, then turned and ran for all I was worth: scampering along fallen logs, leaping over boulders, crashing through brush. Soon I heard panting behind me. I turned to see . . .

"Mademoiselle!" I gasped. "Has something been forgotten?"

"Yes," she said. "Me. You forgot me."

MANY DAYS LATER

We began to be disheartened. Monique and I had been following my crew for days and days. And rather than getting closer, we were falling behind. While they paddled in a straight line, we had many more twisty, turny miles of shoreline to negotiate.

After another day of leaping, jumping, skittering, scampering, climbing, clambering, and flinging ourselves through space, Monique and I sat with our sad heads in our sad paws.

Gray clouds had swallowed up the sun. A breeze kicked the water into restless whitecaps. The waves lapped sadly against the rocky shoreline. The smell of cool water, cold nights, crisp leaves, and fallen pine needles was heavy on the air.

"Fall is coming," Monique said.

"Indeed," I agreed, shivering.

"Dear Le Rouge," Monique said, "we are falling behind. We shall never apprehend them at this rate."

"We must think of something."

"*Monsieur*, you are a little bit nutty, but I love you anyway."

My heart stopped. What did she say? Love?

"But, *mademoiselle*," I said, "here I am, far from home, a miserable failure. I failed at being a voyageur. I failed at convincing the voyageurs the error of their ways. I would have been willing to go home, tail between my legs, a failure. But I failed even at that! I had intended, when I left home, to explore the unexplored, discover the undiscovered, taste the untasted."

"But you have done all that!" Monique protested. "You discovered me. We have explored all along these wild shores, and could explore them more if we slowed down a little. And as for tasting the untasted, try this."

She popped a very tasty something into my mouth—a little nutty, a little fruity, a little salty, a little sweet.

"What was that?" I asked. "I have never tasted anything like it!"

"Now you have tasted the untasted," she said. "Perhaps you should be satisfied."

But I was not.

MORE DAYS PASS IN WHICH
WE CHASE MY CREW

We were now speeding along. I believed we were sure to catch up to the brigade. Monique and I had made a canoe.

Oui, c'est vrai. A canoe.

It was exactly like a real voyageur's canoe—only smaller. Quite a bit smaller.

We had made it from a fallen strip of birch bark, sewn together with strips of willow we had chewed soft. Our paddles we had nibbled from a cedar plank.

Our canoe was beautiful and we loved her as we might love our best friend.

She guided us through the water without a sound.

She weaved through the rapids as if she knew the way.

She kept us dry on rainy nights.

Oui, bien sûr, we loved her!

In the big canoe, I did not paddle. In our small canoe, I paddled! Oh, how I paddled!

And at the portages, I carried my weight. If Monique didn't carry it, I even carried the canoe.

We traveled night and day, stopping only to gather nuts and seeds to stave off hunger. At night we traveled by lantern light. Of course, we always let the fireflies go before they got too tired.

WE LOSE TRACK OF THE TIME

Days went by in a blur of color:
  Red maple leaves.
  Golden tamarack needles.
  Burgundy oak leaves.
  Yellow aspen leaves.
  Waterways in shades of green, aqua, turquoise,
cobalt.
  And the sky on fire with the blaze of sunset.

THERE IS A BIG WIND

I did not know where we were, perhaps on a route of our own devising. We could not make progress because a big wind pushed us backwards across a lake. Our little canoe tossed helplessly on the waves. Snow began to fall.

"*Monsieur,*" said Monique, "*il neige*—it snows."

"*Oui, oui,*" said I. "I see it." How could one have seen anything else? It fell so fast and thick it was like fur.

We paddled to the shore and pulled the canoe up onto the ground.

I stared out into the blinding snow. It piled up and up. Monique wore a tall hat of snow. She shivered and blew on her tiny paws.

"The wind, she howls," Monique said. "The snow, she swirls."

"*Vite!* Quick!" I said. "Turn the boat upside down!" We did so, and I encouraged her to crawl underneath it.

As for me, I stood for a few more moments looking east, wondering how far we were from Montreal. If I had caught up to the brigade, if I had traveled triumphantly into Montreal with them, would I have earned a red cap and a red sash? Perhaps I could have been a voyageur after all? I guess I never really gave up my dream.

But in my heart of hearts I knew that even if I had returned in the voyageurs' canoe, I would not have earned anything. I was not really a voyageur. In the big Montreal canoe, I did not paddle. I did not cook; I only ate. On the portages I did not carry much. Well, I admit, I carried nothing. I understood that they were right and I was wrong. I was not cut out to be a voyageur.

I shook the snow from my fur and crawled under our tiny boat. Monique had made a soft carpet of leaves. She had laid out a fine meal of seeds and dried mushrooms. It was cozy and warm. Outside, the snow piled up, but on top of the canoe, not us. We could hear the wind howl, but not feel its bite. Life was not so bad— Monique was there, curled up and already snoring.

I began to feel very drowsy.

PART III

THE LITTLEST VOYAGEUR

SOMETHING WONDERFUL HAPPENS

In the spring, Monique and I launched our canoe once again. We paddled many days, heading west. Getting back to Montreal was not so important after all.

All along our way, squirrels and chipmunks, mice and voles ran out to greet us.

"What do you carry in your boat?" they asked.

And we told them: We had pine seeds and acorns. Musky mushrooms of many flavors. Dried blueberries and rose hips. The bright fallen feathers of blue jays, redpolls, goldfinches—lovely décor for nests. And for warmth, the cozy down of the geese of Canada.

The animals wanted to trade our exotic fare for the nuts, seeds, fruits, and berries they themselves had gathered. They had seeds from flowers we had never seen. Snail shells filled with sweet maple sap. We traded with them and continued on our way.

One day, after many weeks of travel, Monique and I were on the lakeshore counting hazelnuts when I saw a paddle flashing in the sunlight. But it was only one paddle, and as the canoe grew nearer, I saw that it contained only one person.

You can be sure I did a few somersaults and double flips and a cartwheel or two when I saw who was in the canoe. Why, it was Jean Gentille, paddling alone!

I dashed out onto a branch overhanging the water and called to him. "Jean Gentille! Jean

Gentille! Jean Gentille!" I chattered. (If you say it many times in quick succession you will get an approximation of what it sounded like.)

Jean Gentille looked up, and when he saw me, he smiled. "*Bonjour*, little squirrel," he said.

Little squirrel? Didn't he recognize me?

"It's me, Jean Pierre Petit Le Rouge!" I said emphatically.

"You remind me of a squirrel I once knew quite well," he mused.

Out of sheer frustration I executed a double axel with a tail spiral. Couldn't he see who it was? I? Me? *Moi?*

"That little squirrel sure was a nuisance," he said.

What? My tail sagged. My ears drooped.

"Even so," Jean Gentille continued, "I really liked him. You know, it sounds funny to say, but he might have been the best friend I ever had."

I melted into a puddle of red fur.

"And because of him, I have given up the fur trade," Jean Gentille confided.

I sat up, ears perked. Was it so? Could it be?

Jean Gentille continued, "Should you ever see a squirrel by the name of Le Rouge, tell him that thanks to him I am in a new business now. Look!" He gestured toward the bottom of his canoe.

I took a peek and what did I see? Books! Books of all kinds and descriptions, books on any subject and in any form, including a new genre called the "novel."

"The idea is, you can borrow a book, then when I come by the next time bring it back and get a different one. The trade is a little slow," he said, "but it's picking up. I'm quite sure the book-canoe is going to catch on."

Before Jean Gentille left I wanted to give him a keepsake. Monique had carefully patted and formed and felted my shed fur into a luxurious winter nest for the two of us. I ran to get it and then dropped it into the canoe for him.

He picked it up, examined it, and plunked it upside down upon his head. "A perfect fit!" he proclaimed. "A beautiful red *chapeau*! *Merci beaucoup!*"

Taking up his paddle, he said, "You know . . .

though it seems unlikely, I'd say you were that same pesky but lovable squirrel. Could it be you, Le Rouge?"

My heart was so full, I could only sing. I poured my joy into an aria full of runs and trills, with the kind of coloratura only a few can achieve. My voice echoed across the great north country and, for all I know, may be echoing still.

Jean Gentille paddled away, his hearty laugh joining in to make the sweetest of duets. And then, because he still had the soul of a voyageur, he sang a little, too:

Il y a longtemps que je t'aime
Jamais je ne t'oublierai.

Long have I loved you
Never will I forget you.

Monique and I traveled on. Everywhere we went animals rushed to meet us. They wanted to trade their fruits from the west for our seeds from the east. They offered the sweet rice that grows in northern rivers in exchange for succulent acorns that grow in more temperate climes.

"This is a lucrative business," Monique said to me one day.

"'Lucrative'?" I asked. She uses such big words.

"We are doing well for ourselves," she said. "Look at our boat. It is filled with hazelnuts, acorns, walnuts, dried fruits and berries, warm fur and soft feathers, and other such refinements. The value of these things back east will be high. I think we can travel with a bigger canoe next year."

"A bigger canoe!" I exclaimed. "How can the two of us paddle a bigger canoe?"

Monique just smiled.

SPRING 1795

LIFE IS MAGNIFIQUE!

It has been two years since Monique and I began our adventure, and now we paddle a very large canoe. For we are no longer alone. In fact, our family has grown to be a whole brigade. They are:

Marie Claire
Marie Françoise
Marie Martine
Marie Véronique
Marie Monique
Jean Paul
Jean Baptiste
Jean Henri
Jean Marcel

Jean Jacques
Jean Louis
And the littlest one of all . . .
Jean Gentille.
But you know, although I am no longer the littlest voyageur, I am the happiest. For I travel with a fine brigade. And I am a voyageur!

PRONUNCIATION GUIDE

zh = the sound of the "g" at the end of "garage"

eu = the sound in the middle of "should"

onh = the beginning sound in "on" before you say the "n"

allons-y: ah-lonh-zee
arrêtez: ah-ret-tay
bonjour: bonh-zhour
c'est rien: say ryeh
c'est vrai: say vray
chanteur: shohn-teur
chapeau: shah-poe
chut: shoot
dégradé: day-grah-day

dommage: doh-mahzh

en roulant, ma boule roulant: onh roo-lonh,
    ma boo-leu roo-lonh

et moi: ay mwa

grand portage: gronh por-tahzh

hivernants: ee-vehr-nonh

il neige: eel nehzh

il y a longtemps que je t'aime: eel ya lonh-tonh
    qeu zheu tem-eu

jamais je ne t'oublierai: zha-may zheu neu
    too-blyeu-ray

Jean Claude: zhonh clode

Jean Gentille: zhonh zhonh-tee

Jean Henri: zhonh onh-ree

Jean Jacques: zhonh zhahk

Jean Louis: zhonh loo-ee

Jean Luc: zhonh luke

Jean Méchant: zhonh may-shonh

Jean Paul: zhonh pole

Jean Pierre Petit Le Rouge: zhonh pee-air
    peu-tee leu roozh

la vieille: lah veeyay

mademoiselle: mahd-mwa-zelle

magnifique: mah-nyee-feek

mais non: may nonh

mangeurs de lard: manh-zheur deu lahr

merci beaucoup: mare-see boe-coo

mon bon ami: monh bone ahmee

mon Dieu: monh dyeu

monsieur: meu-sheur

n'est-ce pas?: ness-pah

non: nonh

oui: wee

oui, bien sûr: wee, byeh sur

oui, c'est vrai: wee, say vray

pardonnez-moi: par-don-nay mwa

pièces: pyess

ragoût: rah-goo

rendezvous: rohn-day-voo

sacrebleu!: sah-kre-bleu

tête-à-tête: tet-ah-tet

va-t'en!: vah tonh

vite: veet

voilà: vwah-la

youpe, youpe sur la rivière: yoop, yoop sur lah
    ree-vyaire

Canoe Manned by Voyageurs Passing a Waterfall
by Frances Anne Hopkins

ABOUT VOYAGEURS

From the late seventeenth through mid-nineteenth centuries, voyageurs traveled the waterways of what is now the United States and Canada, transporting and trading goods for furs. Especially desired was beaver fur, used for a variety of hats that were popular in Europe at the time. So great was the demand, in fact, that the beaver nearly succumbed to extinction in North America by the late 1800s.

The life of a voyageur was both difficult and dangerous, suited for strong, hardworking, and (if available) small men who could withstand bitter cold, searing heat, clouds of mosquitoes, and long portages across which they would carry two or more ninety-pound parcels. In crews of six to twelve men, they paddled their sturdy birch-bark canoes fourteen to sixteen hours a day, on waterways large and small, placid or wild, often singing to keep up their rhythm and pace. A good *chanteur* (singer) was paid extra, since the songs helped keep the men paddling forty-five strokes per minute and their heavily laden canoes moving along at about six and a half miles per hour. At this rate they could paddle fifty to ninety miles a day.

The canoes coming from Montreal were thirty-six to forty feet long and six feet wide in the middle. Built of birch bark, cedar, pitch, and spruce roots, the canoes were light and strong and able to carry five thousand pounds of cargo. It likely took several people two weeks or more to build a 36-foot canoe.

It might not seem that paddling and portaging would be the most efficient way of hauling so much cargo 2,400 miles round trip, but at the time of the voyageurs it actually was. There were no roads, no trucks, no airplanes. And although Jean Henri foretells it, the railroad boom in the United States didn't take place until the 1930s.

In the days of our story, the voyageurs would

have been working for the North West Company, and were French-Canadian, Anishinaabeg, and other nationalities. They were either "pork eaters" (the crew we follow), or "winterers" (*hivernants* or northmen). The entire round-trip journey from Lachine (near Montreal) to Grand Portage and back took from four to five months, including a two- to four-week stay at Grand Portage. Winterers used smaller canoes to travel the inland lakes and waterways into the interior of the United States and Canada, where they would spend the winter trading with the native people.

The fur trade would not have existed at all had it not been for the Anishinaabeg, who lived and hunted in these regions. They were the master builders of the birch-bark canoe, and they supplied the furs to make the hats (and other items) that were so popular all over Europe. They also helped keep the *hivernants* and clerks at remote trading posts alive during the long winters by supplying them with fish, game, wild rice, and maple sugar. They traded furs and food for iron kettles, flint and steel, wool blankets and calico cotton, silver jewelry, tobacco, beads, and other goods.

Tragically, some of the things the Europeans brought with them to North America—smallpox, for example—had devastating consequences for the Anishinaabeg and other native North American people. But for a time, the fur trade in this part of the country brought prosperity to everyone engaged in it.

ABOUT JEAN PIERRE PETIT LE ROUGE'S SPEECHES

Some of Le Rouge's speeches are not exactly original. His speech to the voyageurs on page 78 foretells Henry David Thoreau, who in his book *Walden* said, "I went to the woods to live deliberately. . . . I wanted to live deep and suck out all the marrow of life."

On page 95, perhaps inspired by Jean Gentille's readings of Shakespeare, Le Rouge rallies the fur-bearers with a version of Henry V's famous Saint Crispin's Day speech (Act 4, scene 3).

ABOUT RED SQUIRRELS AND
FLYING SQUIRRELS

The trilling chirr of the red squirrel is one of the most distinctive sounds of the north woods. Weighing only seven to twelve ounces (as much as three Mars bars), these tiny squirrels are lively acrobats. At times they seem to be just a streak of red as they scamper along the tallest branches of the big pines collecting pinecones for their food caches. These caches, often underground, hold upwards of two hundred pinecones. Red squirrels have such a keen sense of smell that they can easily locate them even under three feet of snow.

The oldest living line of modern squirrel is the flying squirrel. Although it cannot fly like a bird, it uses the furry, parachute-like membrane that stretches from wrist to ankle to help it glide between trees—with coasting flights recorded at almost three hundred feet. It grows to be around eleven inches long, including the tail, but weighs only two to five ounces. Like other squirrels, it eats nuts, acorns, fungi, and lichens.

Both the northern flying squirrel and the red squirrel live in evergreen forests across Canada and the top of the continental United States.

If you are ever in the north country, and you hear a happy chirr coming from a pine tree, look up. If you see a flash of red, it is likely that you have seen one of the great-great-great-great-great-grandchildren of Jean Pierre Petit Le Rouge, the littlest voyageur.

RECISE FOR BANNOCK

1/2 tsp. salt
2 Tbsp. baking powder*
2 cups flour
2 Tbsp. shortening (You can use butter, margarine, bacon fat, or oil.)
2 cups water or milk

Mix together the flour, baking powder, and salt.

Cut in the shortening with a couple of forks, knives, or fingers until mixed in.

Make a "lake" in the middle of the flour mixture and pour the water or milk into the lake, then stir together to make a sticky dough. If you want to handle the dough with your hands, add more flour.

If you're cooking on a fire or stove top, fry biscuit-sized patties in oil on both sides until done. Dough can also be wrapped around a clean stick and toasted over the fire like a marshmallow. Add more flour to make a less-sticky dough.

If you have an oven, spread dough in a greased cast-iron fry pan or eight-inch round or square cake pan and bake at 350° F until done.

* The voyageurs didn't have baking powder, so they didn't use any leavening. You can leave the baking powder out for a more authentic experience.

SOURCES

*RECOMMENDED FOR YOUNG READERS

Amb, Thomas M. *The Voyageurs: Frontiersmen of the Northwest*. Minneapolis: T. S. Denison, 1973.

*Durbin, William. *The Broken Blade*. New York: Delacorte, 1997.

*——. *Wintering*. 2nd ed. Ely, MN: Raven Productions, 2009.

Green, Ellen B. *Fur Trade*. Roots, vol. 10, no. 1. St. Paul: Minnesota Historical Society, 1981.

Huck, Barbara. *Exploring the Fur Trade Routes of North America: Discover the Highways that Opened a Continent*. Winnipeg: Heartland, 2002.

Morse, Eric W. *Fur Trade Canoe Routes of Canada: Then and Now*. 2nd edition. Toronto: University of Toronto Press, 1985.

National Park Service. *Rendezvous with History: A Grand Portage Story* (film). Denver: Great Divide Pictures, 2012.

Nelson, George. *My First Years in the Fur Trade: The Journals of 1802–1804*. Edited by Laura Peers and Theresa Schenck. St. Paul: Minnesota Historical Society Press, 2002.

Nute, Grace Lee. *The Voyageur's Highway: Minnesota's Border Lake Land*. St. Paul: Minnesota Historical Society Press, 1941.

*Peterson, Cris. *Birchbark Brigade: A Fur Trade History*. Honesdale, PA: Calkins Creek, 2009.

Podruchny, Carolyn. *Making the Voyageur World: Travelers and Traders in the North American Fur Trade*. Lincoln: University of Nebraska Press, 2006.

Sivertson, Howard. *The Illustrated Voyageur: Paintings and Companion Stories*. Duluth, MN: Lake Superior Port Cities, 1999.